For Andy

A Random House Australia book
Published by Random House Australia Pty Ltd
Level 3, 100 Pacific Highway, North Sydney NSW 2060
www.randomhouse.com.au

First published by Random House Australia in 2016

Random House Books is part of the Penguin Random House group of companies whose addresses can be found at global.penguinrandomhouse.com.

National Library of Australia
Cataloguing-in-Publication Entry

Author: Bound, Samantha-Ellen
Title: Rhythm and blues
ISBN: 978 0 85798 907 9 (pbk)
Series: Silver shoes; 7
Target Audience: For primary-school age
Subjects: Dance – Juvenile fiction
          Girls – Juvenile fiction
Dewey Number: A823.4

Internal illustrations by Sarah Kate Mitchell
Cover design by Kirby Armstrong
Internal design by Midland Typesetters
Printed in Australia by Griffin Press, an accredited ISO AS/NZS 14001:2004 Environmental Management System printer

Random House Australia uses papers that are natural, renewable and recyclable products and made from wood grown in sustainable forests. The logging and manufacturing processes are expected to conform to the environmental regulations of the country of origin.

Rhythm and Blues

SAMANTHA-ELLEN BOUND

RANDOM HOUSE AUSTRALIA

Chapter One

I don't know how it happened.

One minute I was reaching for the ball, the goalpost in my sight, and the next I was down on the sticky floor, staring at everyone's sneakers, the ball bouncing away from me.

I felt a weird sensation in my lower leg, like a balloon full of pins had burst inside my ankle. Then WHAM! my head smacked into the ground.

Never was I more thankful for my nana's thick, tight braids ('Nana' is what I call my mum; it's a term from Fiji, which is where I'm from). I'm sure they cushioned the blow.

Blackness flooded my vision for a second. I blinked it away and let my eyes swim back into focus. There was a crowd of girls peering down at me.

'Let me through, let me through!' My basketball coach, Stacey, pushed the players aside and knelt down next to me.

'Riley?' she said. 'Are you okay? Did you hit your head? What happened?'

I coughed and tried to sit up, but little stars danced across the insides of my eyelids. A queasy feeling was making a whirlwind in my guts. I wished everyone would back away because they were making me feel worse.

Talk about embarrassing.

'I jumped to catch the ball,' I managed to say. 'And then I landed on my foot wrong. It kind of rolled?'

'Does it hurt now?' asked Stacey.

'Not too badly,' I said, although the sensation of a million pins stabbing into your ankle probably wasn't that healthy.

I never get injured. I was mad at myself and my body for letting me down, and causing this stupid scene in the middle of the court.

'Sit up when you're ready,' Stacey said. 'We'll get you off the court and bring you some ice to put on it.' She looked at my head. 'And for your noggin, too. You might have concussion.'

'I don't have anything,' I said, and to prove that, I took a breath and sat up. My eyes went swirly and my stomach along with them, but after a second the feeling went away.

Stacey glared at me. 'Riley, I said when you were *ready*.'

'I am ready,' I lied. 'Get me off this court.'

Stacey reached under me and put her arm around my back to hoist me up. I almost died. One of my friends, Ellie, would have loved the attention. She would even have thrown in some fake faints! My other best friend, Ash, would have laughed it off and made a joke about being a klutz. But I knew my third best friend, Paige, would have felt exactly the same as I did. I wished she was here right now instead of all these strangers smothering me.

'Riley, don't go so fast,' Stacey scolded me.

I was just about pulling her along the court towards our team seats. My head was swimming and I felt like my breakfast might come back up. But I just had to get off that court, and away from all the attention.

Thankfully, I heard the whistle blow behind me, which meant the game had started again.

Opal, the girl subbing for me, held out her hand for a high five as she raced on.

I gave it a weak slap but really I was super annoyed at her for taking my place.

'Sit on the ground, Riley, and put your foot up on this.' Stacey carefully placed her backpack under my injured foot. The assistant coach, Jackson, handed her two ice packs, each wrapped in a towel. 'Put this on your ankle, too. You might have a sprain. Whack this other one on where you hit your head. Jackson will sit with you to make sure you're okay.'

'Is this really necessary?' I grumbled, trying to wave Jackson away. 'I'm fine. I can barely even feel it.' In truth, both my ankle and head felt like they were on fire, but I just needed to sit by myself for a few minutes and I'd be okay.

'Probably 'cause you've got concussion,' Jackson said.

'Put your jacket on, too,' Stacey said. 'Keep warm. Don't let yourself get cold.'

'But I'm going back on in a minute!' I protested.

Stacey stared at me. 'Riley,' she said, 'you are not playing for the rest of the game.'

'What!' I went to stand up but didn't quite get there.

'Case in point,' Stacey said. 'The St John Ambulance man is going to check in on you in a second. You have to sit the rest of the game out. Otherwise you'll do more damage than good.'

'I can tell you some really cool jokes in the meantime,' Jackson offered, but I was too disappointed to even pretend to laugh.

I hate sitting out on anything. All I could think was that my stupid ankle better be fine by tomorrow, because there was no way I was going to miss my dance classes at Silver Shoes.

Chapter Two

Silver Shoes is the dance school Ellie, Paige and I have been going to since we were tinies. Ash joined us at the start of the year – she came from our enemy school, Dance Art Academy. But I think we all agree she's way happier here!

I had a lyrical class at Silver Shoes on Saturday morning – the day after my little accident at basketball. There was absolutely no way I could afford to miss it – especially with our exams coming up in a few weeks. Plus, I really love lyrical. Ballet is my main style, but I started doing lyrical a couple of years ago when Ellie told me I was too serious and needed to try a style where I could let my feelings out. It's amazing how lyrical lets you express yourself in a way that ballet doesn't (even if sometimes I struggle with really 'letting go'!).

I didn't tell my family that I'd hurt my ankle or slammed my head into the ground. My big brother Fergus picks me up and he never comes into the stadium; he always waits outside near his car so he can whistle at any girls who walk by. (He doesn't seem to notice or care that they snort in laughter and roll their eyes).

The ambulance man had wrapped a bandage around my ankle, told me to keep icing it, and not do any vigorous exercise for a few days. So there was no getting around that. But I just told Nana and Tata (that's 'Dad' in Fijian) that it was there because I'd landed a bit funny out of a jump. I said nothing at all about my 'concussion', even though I felt a bit woozy right up until I went to bed.

Are you wondering why I didn't say anything? Well, it's because I knew I'd be all right. I didn't want any fuss and to be stopped from going to dance class just because I'd hurt my ankle a bit.

I didn't need people telling me things about my body when it seemed to me that I was the best judge of it and what it was capable of doing.

And missing a dance class so close to exams was not an option. We only did exams once a year, and this year my age group were doing our Silver Shoes Level Three exams in jazz, tap, musical theatre, ballet and lyrical – whatever classes we took. If we didn't pass, we wouldn't be able to move up to the next level – which would be embarrassing, but it'd also be a waste of all the time and effort we'd put in to get better.

So, with that on my mind, I cruised into lyrical class on Saturday morning like nothing had ever happened. I made sure I wore thick leg warmers over my ankles so our teacher, Miss Caroline, wouldn't see the bandage on my right foot.

And I tried to ignore the little niggling pain in my ankle that insisted this wasn't a good idea.

'Hey Riley, how'd you go at basketball last night?'

Paige took her place next to me before warm-up, which is how we start every class, followed by travelling exercises, and then a short routine. At this time of year, we also spend half an hour at the end of class running through our upcoming exams.

'We lost,' I said, rolling my ankle around in circles to see where the pain was.

'Oh, I'm sorry,' said Paige. She gave me a sweet smile, which made her look even more doll-like than usual. Today she'd pulled two bits of hair out of her tight blonde bun, and they curled around her face. I gave one a playful tug.

'Doesn't matter,' I said. 'It's the off-season. It's only meant to be a bit of fun after the main season.' (Which, I might add, my team won.)

Paige said something else but I was concentrating on my ankle, silently willing it to get through this class and not make a fool of me. It didn't feel 100 per cent great, but if I took it easy I should be okay.

'Riley?' asked Paige.

'Huh?' I said.

She gave me a strange look. 'Are you okay?'

'Yeah, of course,' I said.

'Well, what I was saying,' she continued, 'is that after Ellie finishes rehearsal today, she wants to know if we can meet Ash at Groove Train for ice-cream.'

Ellie is in a musical at the moment called *Mary Poppins*, and they rehearse over in Silver Shoes' drama studio. It's actually just after our exams that they'll have their opening night.

'Oh,' I said. 'Yeah, sure. Sounds good.'

That's if I didn't put myself in the hospital first.

Chapter Three

Miss Caroline arrived to begin class. I guess I got lucky because our lyrical warm-ups aren't very energetic or cardio-based, like our jazz ones.

Lyrical warm-ups focus on movements that have a natural, flowing feel to them. There are a lot of swings, isolations, contractions and long stretches to get your blood pumping. So I handled those pretty well, keeping as much weight as I could off my bad ankle and cheating in some of the stretches.

Although I did notice Paige looking at me a bit suspiciously when I didn't go as far into my lunges as I usually do. She knows I give it my all in class every single time, no matter if it's warm-up, travelling, or choreography work. I hate doing anything when I know, with less laziness, I could have done better. Ellie is a bit the same, I guess, which is why we get on, even though we're both so different.

I gave Paige a bright smile like I had no idea why she would think anything was wrong, but even so I hurried over to the corner when it came time for travelling work. I could tell it was on the tip of her tongue to ask if there was something up with my ankle, and I didn't want anyone, not even Paige, to know I was dancing when perhaps I shouldn't be.

It could only last so long, though.

Travelling steps proved my downfall.

I figured out pretty quick that there was no pretending when it came to posé turns and saut de basque jumps. Even simple lyrical travelling steps like a waltz, tombé or pas de bourrée were a struggle. Putting any sort of weight on my ankle became a real problem, and eventually it began to hurt so much that when I was landing jumps and leaps, I started to flinch.

All the time I could feel Paige's eyes on me, watching very, very carefully. I couldn't help it, though. I kept pushing. I prided myself on my technical steps and setting an example for the other girls. I felt like a failure if I sat out or started doing the exercises with half my usual energy.

'Riley,' Paige said to me, as I lined up to do my turning jetés. 'Is your foot okay? Because you shouldn't be . . .'

I took off then, before she could finish, in case anyone else could hear. But because I was in such a hurry to get away, I mucked up my timing and messed up my preparation for the turn leap.

Then it happened.

I turned, leapt, landed . . . and it felt like someone had just smashed a branch into my ankle. I stumbled, tried to right myself, half fell and half lowered my body to the floor. Pain flared up my leg from my ankle.

I had a very, very bad feeling that I'd just made everything a hundred times worse.

Chapter Four

I bit my lip. My ankle hurt so badly.

Do not cry, Riley, do not cry.

'Riley!' Paige yelled, breaking away from the corner and rushing over to me. A few busybody girls followed her.

I had to get out of the room. I absolutely could not have a repeat of yesterday.

Paige flung herself down next to me. 'I *knew* something was wrong!' she exclaimed. 'Is it your ankle?'

The other girls arrived at the scene and Miss Caroline pushed through them. 'Give her some space,' she said, gently. 'Riley? What's happened? Did you land funny?'

'I . . . I . . .' I hung my head and clutched at my ankle, trying to stop the flares of pain from running up my shin. 'I hurt it a little at basketball and then I put too much weight on it and . . . and . . .' I grimaced. 'It really hurts!'

Miss Caroline looked at me and I felt like she knew everything that was going on in my head, including that I felt like the world's biggest dummy.

'Okay, Riley,' she said, and gave a brisk clap. 'Girls, that's enough, return to the corner. Bethany, you run and get Jay – he's on the reception desk today – and tell him to come and carry Riley out to my office. Paige, you want to go with them?'

Paige nodded very seriously, her long lashes blinking back her own tears.

Miss Caroline knelt down next to me while everyone else but Paige went back to the corner.

'She probably did it on purpose,' I heard one girl, Jasmine, mutter. 'For the attention.'

Jasmine is a great dancer but she's also pretty snobby. She and her sidekick, Tove, are always making life difficult for me and my friends. It was just like Jasmine to say something like that, and stupid too, because *as if* I wanted everyone eyeballing me while I was sprawled on the ground.

But my ankle hurt too much to even think about saying something snappy back to her.

'Can you put weight on it?' Miss Caroline asked.

I shook my head. I knew I couldn't. It was

ten times worse than at basketball. I was really afraid I'd done something serious.

'You've probably got a sprain, judging by the way you landed,' Miss Caroline said. 'We'll keep it elevated and ice it here, but I'll get Jay to call your parents to come pick you up. I recommend you go to the doctor, honey, especially if you had a problem with it before class.'

I nodded miserably and wished the walls of Silver Shoes would tumble down around me. 'I'm sorry, Miss Caroline,' I whispered. 'I just didn't want to miss today's lesson, not with exams so close.'

Miss Caroline gave a kind chuckle and squeezed my arm. 'I understand,' she said. 'Your commitment is fantastic. But you should never put your health at risk. You only had to tell me and I would have let you modify everything – or you even could have watched along with me to keep the steps in your memory. It isn't a weakness to give your body a rest every now and then.'

Paige put her arms around me. 'Riley is very stubborn,' she said, 'but that's why we love her. She always gives everything 100 per cent, Miss Caroline.'

Miss Caroline nodded at my ankle. 'Well, let's just hope you make a 100 per cent recovery from this.'

Jay dashed in then, making ambulance noises. He's the hip hop teacher at Silver Shoes. Everyone has a crush on him because he's young and funny and has terrific shaggy hair. Not me, though. Having three older brothers makes you allergic to boys!

'Doctor Jay to the rescue,' he joked, pretend-driving to me. 'Heard you got yourself an injury, Riles? You okay, chicky? You need ol' Jay to give you a leg up?'

I nodded.

'Woo!' Jay teased. 'Not even a comeback from the young lady! This must be serious!'

That, at least, made me smile.

'Come on,' Jay said. 'Hang onto my arm there, that's it.' I put all my weight on my left leg as he helped me upright. 'Now I get to sweep you off your feet.' He grinned and, to my total embarrassment, lifted me up so I was being carried off like some princess in a fairytale.

Poor Paige gave an embarrassed giggle for me as Jay tipped her a wink.

'It's how I get all the ladies,' he said. 'Right! Let's go get some ice and make some calls. The health and wellbeing of Madam's dainty foot depends on it!'

But I had a feeling that my injury was a lot more serious than his jokiness let on.

Chapter Five

'You're not supposed to dance for three weeks?'
Ellie flung herself back on my bed, kicking
her legs up. Her pink sneaker pumps almost
hit me in the face. She widened her green
eyes dramatically and clutched at her heart.
'I would die!'

'And even then, when the three weeks is
up, I'll still have to take it easy for a while and
not do anything too "strenuous".' I stared

glumly at my foot, which was propped up on two pillows and covered with a bag of frozen corn.

The girls had come round to my house Tuesday afternoon, a few days after my fall at Silver Shoes, and I was delivering them the news:

I, Riley Nason, had a sprained ankle.

In other words, my life as I knew it was over.

At least for a couple of weeks.

Ashley looked over from where she was trying on my collection of hats in the mirror. 'I'm sorry, Riles,' she said. 'Does that mean you have to miss some basketball games too?'

'Yeah,' I said. 'And the track meet next month.' I punched my spare pillow and scowled at the frozen corn. 'What am I going to do? I can't just sit around at home all day! I already missed ballet on Monday night. I'm going to fall behind!'

'You can play with Del?' suggested Paige, who was sitting on the floor, holding my baby sister, Del, and making cute faces at her.

Paige is an only child, so she loves playing with Del or Ellie's little brother, Lucas. She's great with them, too. Sometimes I think they like her more than us!

'Del's cool,' I said, giving my sister a smile, which she returned with her crooked baby teeth. 'But she spends most of the day sleeping.'

'Ugh!' Ashley joked. 'I'd love to spend all day sleeping! Maybe we can swap places?'

'I'd swap places with anyone who had a working ankle,' I said.

'Even Jasmine?' asked Ellie, fluffing out her blonde curls as she lay down next to me and reached for one of Nana's coconut sugar cookies.

Ashley giggled. 'You'd get a working ankle but an empty brain instead.'

'Be nice,' Paige warned. 'Riley, what happened after you left Silver Shoes on Saturday? Did you go straight to the doctor?'

'Yeah,' I said. 'Nana took me. The doctor made me move my ankle in different ways, and he poked and prodded at it and all the time it was growing to the size of a watermelon! Then I had to get an X-ray. They made me take my jewellery off and then wear this weird apron thing.'

'That's why I will never allow myself to get sick or injured,' said Ellie. 'Hospitals are so unfashionable.'

'The price you pay when you're saving lives,' Ashley said, playfully throwing a cap at Ellie, who lunged to protect the sugar cookies. 'You'd probably add rhinestones to your hospital smock.'

'Anyway,' I interrupted, 'we got the results back and I have a sprained ankle. The doctor said it's bordering on Grade Two, which is like in the middle of how bad a sprained ankle can be. So if I keep this compression bandage on it and ice it twice a day for at least a week, then after a few more weeks I can slowly get back into dancing and all that.'

'Did the doctor give you instructions on how to care for it and the strengthening exercises you should do daily?' Paige asked. 'I remember when my mum hurt her ankle at the gym and she got this booklet on rehabilitation. It really helped her.'

'Yeah, he did,' I said, shrugging at a pile of papers I'd dumped by the side of my bed. 'I haven't really looked at them, though. Whatever. It isn't exactly hard to keep my weight off my foot and do some pointing and flexing.'

'But he gave them to you for a reason,' Paige insisted. 'You should at least check them out. There must be something in there that'll help.'

'I know how to look after my own body, Paige!' I snapped.

She looked at me in surprise and then turned to Del, picking at one of the buttons on her baby smock.

Ellie sat up and glared at me angrily. She gets really defensive over Paige, and I knew that if she was giving me her 'Ellie' look, I'd gotten a bit out of line.

I sighed. 'I'm sorry,' I said. 'I didn't mean to be mean, Paige. I'm just disappointed. And annoyed at myself for doing this. And . . . worried. Exams are so close. It's just the worst time to get an injury.'

'Urst!' agreed Del.

Paige smiled and smoothed my baby sister's hair. 'That's all right,' she said, 'I understand. But we'll help you if we can. And you're so fit and strong, Riley. I'm sure you'll be back to your best in no time.'

'Hear, hear,' agreed Ashley. She deepened her voice. 'Coming to a cinema near you: *Riley's Return*. How one girl dared to jeté where no girl had jetéd before.' She came up and slung one of my caps on my head. 'Come in to jazz tomorrow, yeah? Just to sit and watch. It might make you feel better. Miss Caroline won't mind.'

I screwed up my nose. Sitting and watching everyone else dance didn't sound like much fun. But being at Silver Shoes always made me feel good. Maybe the key to a healthy ankle was a happy heart?

I'd give it a try.

Chapter Six

It wasn't a nice feeling hobbling into Silver Shoes the next day on a crutch. I was supposed to use it for a couple of weeks to help me get around and to keep the weight off my ankle.

Even trying to get up the few front steps and inside was an effort – I almost broke a sweat! My armpit ached from where the crutch was tucked in under it. But I didn't let anyone help me. My ankle might be out for a few weeks, but it didn't mean I couldn't do things for myself!

Anyway, I got to the top of the dratted stairs and stood in the foyer of Silver Shoes (which is really just the old entrance to the church the building used to be). I felt very overwhelmed, like there was some sludgy muck pushing in on me at every side and I couldn't move.

'Afternoon, Riley,' sang Mrs de Lacy, the main receptionist at Silver Shoes, who also happens to be Jasmine's mum. Jasmine was there, too. She gave me a good looking over.

I pushed away the sludge and flicked my two braids back. Then I straightened my body over the crutch. I would never let Jasmine see how much this stupid ankle was getting me down.

I don't know if it was because her mum was there, but Jasmine didn't have anything mean or gloating to say. In fact, I'm pretty sure there was something like a sympathetic smile taking over her lips.

'I heard about your ankle,' Jasmine said. 'I'm sorry. It must be really frustrating.'

'Uh . . . thanks.' There was an awkward pause, so I just blundered through to studio one.

Jasmine being nice was almost as weird as Paige being nasty!

I didn't want her pity, though. It made me more determined than ever to get my ankle in working order again.

When I got to studio one, I waved at Ellie, Ash and Paige, then went to sit down at the side of the room. Miss Caroline gave me a big, encouraging smile as I plonked my bum on the seat and threw the horrible crutch to the floor.

'Good to see you, Riley,' she said. 'Let me know if you need anything.'

'Got a new ankle?' I joked.

Miss Caroline laughed. 'Honey, mine aren't much better,' she said.

At first it was sort of fun to watch from the side. My whole perspective of the class changed when I was observing it and not actually in it, working with my brain in dance mode.

I saw how Ellie cheated a little to push herself into side splits, by letting her feet roll in. I admired Jasmine and how her flat back stretches were so straight I could have balanced marbles along her spine. And I noticed, for the first time, how Serah always confirmed she had the right alignment by watching Jasmine, and adjusting her lines off Little Miss Perfect.

But then I started to fidget. My ankle ached. The hair that always falls out of my braids began to prickle my neck in the most annoying way. I got angry at myself for sitting there like a slob when I could be dancing like the other girls.

And then I got angry when they had trouble doing a lame duck turn or a barrel jump and I knew I could have been up there, executing them perfectly, and feeling all the wonderful power and grace that comes with your body poking its tongue out at the laws of gravity.

The worst part was when it came time for exam practice. Exams are divided into four sections – standing warm-up, floor warm-up, travelling steps, and a short routine where you show off both your technique and your performance. I tried to concentrate really hard, watching the sequences and moves closely, committing them to memory, but I got confused when my body wasn't actually moving along with my mind.

I couldn't do this.

'Toilet break,' I whispered to Miss Caroline as I struggled up out of the seat. The stupid crutch got caught on a leg of the chair and fell to the ground with a giant clatter, and of course, everyone stopped and looked.

I gritted my teeth, hauled it up and hobbled to the door.

'Did someone let a pirate loose?' I heard Jasmine whisper loudly.

'You okay?' Ash mouthed at me, but I just shook my head and didn't stop moving until I was safe in the emptiness of studio two.

There I closed the door and leaned against it, sucking in breaths.

'You're not beating me, you stupid ankle,' I said out loud, and pushed myself off the door and into the middle of the room.

I tried to balance on one foot and go through what I remembered of the warm-up part of the exam. But as soon as I put weight on my right foot, my ankle gave a warning throb and my leg buckled. Only the crutch saved me from falling to the floor.

'Dumb thing!' I yelled at the crutch, and threw it across the room.

The sound the crutch made as it clattered and bounced against the floor was just as if it were laughing.

Chapter Seven

I woke up the next morning, hoping that my ankle had miraculously healed and that when I sprang out of bed I would land on it and . . .

Nope. A quick shift of weight while I sat on the edge of my bed revealed my ankle was as sprained and sore as ever.

It took all I had to not crawl under my sheets and throw the covers over my head.

My ankle even made being at school hard. I don't go to the same schools as Ellie, Paige, or Ash. I'm at this private school, St Vitus, which unfortunately a lot of the Dance Art girls go to. Luckily I have my own group of cool friends there, but I couldn't really hang out with them at lunch. We always rig up some kind of game on the basketball courts or walk around the playground, and even that was too tiring and uncomfortable for me.

Instead, I got special permission to access the library at lunch, where I spent my whole time googling or looking up in old books the best way to speed up recovery from a sprained ankle.

But after school was the worst. I had a snack. I did my homework. And then I absolutely died! I couldn't go to dancing, I couldn't go to basketball training, I couldn't go out riding my bike, and I could barely even play chasey in the backyard with Del!

I flicked on the television. Boring.

I scanned through my brother's DVD collection. Too lame.

I braided my hair, and after that I braided Del's. Then I had to take hers out because she cried (I think I did it too tight).

I flopped around on the couch. I picked up the pamphlets the doctor had given me on ankle exercises and barely even looked at them before flinging them back down.

The house was suffocating me! It was my fifth afternoon at home since I'd sprained my ankle and I honestly thought I would just melt into a puddle of frustration if I didn't get out soon.

I needed to be moving; I needed to be learning, to have my mind engaged. Dancing was my escape!

But what could I do?

'I hate you!' I screamed at my ankle.

My brother Fergus poked his head around the door. 'Geez,' he said. 'What now? I used air freshener in the toilet and everything.'

'Not you!' I said. 'My ankle! I'm so bored. I hate sitting around! This is the worst thing that could happen to me. And my ankle's itchy, Ferg! I can't even scratch it because of all these stupid bandages. I hate everything!' I covered my head with a pillow.

Fergus laughed. 'What a performance,' he said, taking the pillow and bopping me lightly with it. 'You in the running for an Academy Award or what? You know, if you hate everything, that means you hate me, and if you hate me, I can't be a good big brother and drive you somewhere that might help you out of your current mood, now, can I?' Fergus tickled the bottom of my good foot with the pillow. 'Can I, Riles?'

'Get off!' I kicked at him, but he ducked it easily. 'You can't take me places anyway, because I can't do anything. I'm like a . . . a plank of wood.'

'Why don't you go visit your dance school and hang around, see your friends?' Fergus suggested. 'That will make you feel better.'

'I did that yesterday and I hated it,' I said. 'It was really frustrating and annoying to watch everyone else dance when I can't. They kept making mistakes. I felt like I should be teaching them.'

'Well, why don't you do what your mate Ash does, and find some odd jobs around the place?' Fergus said. 'Just while you get better. Ash seems to like it. Maybe you can help out at reception or something.'

'Maybe,' I sighed.

'Come on, Little Miss Grump,' he said. 'Besides, I have to go by Silver Shoes on my way to Dylan's. I'll give you a lift and pick you up when I drive home.'

'Hmmmm –' I drawled out. 'I don't know.'

Fergus whacked me with the pillow. 'Up you get!' He laughed. 'Come on, ol' Peg Leg, your ship leaves in five minutes. If you're not there by then, I'll start charging a waiting fee.'

'You should pay me for even getting into your bomb, oh whoops, I mean car,' I said, but I got up.

Fergus was right. I had to get out of the house. And maybe I could find a use for myself at Silver Shoes that didn't directly involve dance.

Anything was better than being a couch potato.

Chapter Eight

Silver Shoes was quiet when I arrived. I could hear a class in studio two but no one else seemed to be around. Technique class was at five o' clock, so I'd see all my friends then, but what was I meant to do in the meantime?

I clod-hopped past reception, turned right and went down the hall that ran along the side of the two main studios. The side that didn't look onto the studios was lined with framed pictures and posters, and up the nearest end to reception was the Silver Shoes noticeboard. I studied it all, hoping for inspiration about what I might be able to do for the next few weeks while my ankle healed.

I peeped through the viewing window that looked in on studio two. The juniors were in there, learning a jazz routine. The sight of them having fun and jumping around so easily made my heart twinge. They had huge smiles on their faces and I understood how they felt, but I couldn't imagine feeling like that myself with an ankle the size of a bouncing castle.

Next I poked around the back of Silver Shoes, studying the props and costume rooms, which were looking pretty spick and span thanks to Ashley's work cleaning them. Maybe I could do that, too?

But I didn't want to take away from Ashley's job. I knew that doing it helped her pay for her beloved hip hop lessons at Silver Shoes and I would never ruin that for her.

I kept trudging on through the dark, sweet-smelling hallways, past the change rooms and Miss Caroline's office and then the teachers' room, where they all hang out when they don't have to teach.

'Riley!' a voice called to me through the open door.

I stopped. 'Yes?'

'Come in here a minute, would you?' Miss Caroline poked her head around the door, a steaming mug of coffee in her hand.

'Sure,' I said.

I wondered if I was in trouble for leaving jazz class so suddenly yesterday. Miss Caroline had been doing me a favour by letting me watch the lesson, and I guess it had been a bit rude when I stormed out.

I inched through the open doorway, trying

46

not to look around and make a big deal about being in the teachers' room. It's kind of a forbidden, unknown territory to students.

I mean, really, it was just an old room with peeling wallpaper and a giant ballerina rug, some old couches covered in colourful throws, with a few coffee tables and a little kitchen.

'Come and have a seat.' Miss Caroline patted the couch opposite her. 'Would you like some cake? Billie brought it in today. She makes the most delicious sweets.'

'Um . . . thank you.' I took a slice, more to be polite than anything. Then I put it in a napkin on my lap and picked at it with my fingers.

'How are you doing, Riley? How's the ankle?' Miss Caroline took a sip of her coffee. 'Ick,' she said, making a face. 'Instant.'

'My ankle? Well, you know, still not working.' I studied a crumb and popped it into my mouth.

My gaze wandered around the room. I didn't want to look Miss Caroline in the eyes because I knew I would get upset and she'd see how down I really was. I don't like to show my feelings, much. I think I get it from Tata. That doesn't mean I don't have them, though!

'That must be very frustrating,' Miss Caroline said, 'for a girl with your ambition and dedication and, dare I say, competitiveness.' Her eyes twinkled at me over the steam of her coffee. With her hair in a long plait, she looked much younger than I knew she was.

'Yeah,' I agreed. 'I don't like sitting around on my bum, er, backside, that's for sure. But I'm also really worried about exams. I felt I was totally prepared for them, and now I don't even know if my ankle will be healed in time.'

'Don't worry about that,' Miss Caroline said. 'If worst comes to worst, I'll make an allowance that you can sit your exams at a later date to everyone else. But I'm sure that if you follow your doctor's instructions and rest your ankle properly, you'll be just fine.'

'Thank you, Miss Caroline,' I said. I scraped at some icing with my finger.

'But –' Miss Caroline sat back on the couch '– what to do while we wait for this ankle to heal, hmm?'

I looked down at my cake.

'I may have a proposition for you, Riley,' she said.

For the first time in almost a week, I felt a little flare of hope. 'Yes?' I said.

'It's going to be hectic coming into exams and also the end-of-year performance,' Miss Caroline said. She held up her mug. 'Even finding time to sit down to have a cuppa is hard these days. I could really use a personal assistant, someone to help me out. To be my extra set of eyes in class and to take exam groups when I'm busy with another; maybe even run a few errands for me? Is that something you'd like to do, Riley?'

'Yes!' I said. 'Yes, yes, yes!' I leaned forward and only just caught the slice of cake in time to prevent it from a mushy death on the rug.

'Well, consider yourself hired!' Miss Caroline laughed. 'Welcome to the staff of Silver Shoes, Riley Nason.'

Chapter Nine

My first job for Miss Caroline was to print off the exam running sheets. That was what the examiners would use to mark us when they came to Silver Shoes. You see, the studio doesn't use teachers from our own school to take the exams. I guess it's because they might show favouritism, or because they already know us, so it's hard to judge us based on just what they see in the exam.

Miss Caroline gave me a USB stick and told me to go into her office and print five copies each of the jazz, ballet, lyrical, tap and musical theatre sheets, on the official Silver Shoes paper. Then I was to bring some to Miss Caroline for her to use in our practice, and file the rest away in the 'exam correspondence' pigeonhole at the front desk.

I chanted the instructions in my head as I hobbled to her office. I knew Miss Caroline had given me a big responsibility, and it was a privilege – I didn't want to stuff it up. She was being super kind to me and I was determined to be the best personal assistant she'd ever had. I was really grateful to her for giving me something to take my mind off not being able to dance for a while.

Miss Caroline's office smelled like the lily-of-the-valley perfume she always wore. I couldn't stop a little giggle as I made my way across the thick cream carpet and took my place at the chair behind her desk.

'Why, yes, my dear, won't you step into my office?' I said out loud, then quickly peeped out the door in case anyone had heard me. I still felt like I was in an out-of-bounds area, doing something wrong. It was a funny, thrilling feeling. I was a bit giddy with it.

I logged onto her computer as 'Guest' and plugged the USB in. The computer whirred and blinked as it loaded the device. Then a folder came up with a bunch of files. There were icons for the five exams – jazz, ballet, lyrical, tap and musical theatre.

There were also two other icons. One said 'Minutes and Stats from Audit Outcome' (which sounded like the most boring thing in the universe). The other was a sub-folder that said 'Notes for Exam Practice – Students by Alphabetical Order'.

I hovered the mouse over it for a second, wondering if I could just take a passing glance to see what it was.

But the title already made it pretty clear what was inside. And I also knew that they were Miss Caroline's private files and none of my business.

A good personal assistant wasn't a snoop.

I quickly clicked into the first exam icon, jazz, and opened it up. There were four pages listing the exam groups and then the criteria we were marked against – technique, style, alignment, memory, placement – with spaces to put notes, crosses and ticks.

I only hoped, when the time came, my injured ankle didn't earn me more crosses than ticks.

I loaded the special Silver Shoes paper into the printer, taking great care to make sure they were all lined up exactly.

Then, while I waited for the next exam sheet to print, I carefully arranged and clipped everything together, taking note of the exam groups while I did so.

Exams were ordered alphabetically, with four people to a group. Because Ellie's last name is Irvin and Ashley's is Jenkyns, they were in the same group for all the classes they were in together. I knew they would be happy about that – it's always nice to know you've got a friend with you.

In my exams – ballet, jazz and lyrical – I was with Paige, because our last names, Montreal and Nason, were close together. Usually I like being with Paige because she gets so nervous and I think having me there is comforting to her. But I knew I would be frazzled this time around, and I didn't want to let her down. I couldn't be strong for others if I couldn't even be strong for myself.

I felt very official walking out of the office with the papers stacked under my arm. After I dropped off the extra copies to reception, I headed down to technique class, which was just starting.

'Here you are, Miss Caroline,' I whispered to her.

She looked down at me and stopped the girls in the middle of their tendu practice. 'Thank you very much,' she said to me before turning to the class. 'Girls, for the next couple of weeks Riley is going to be my personal assistant.'

I held my head high and tried to stand very straight, which was a bit difficult while leaning on a crutch.

'I'm sure you'll all agree that there couldn't be a better person for the job. And I know you won't slack off with her either, or she'll pass that information straight on to me, won't you, Riley?'

'Yes, I will,' I said very seriously, as I looked out at the girls who were to be my sort-of students for the next few weeks.

Most of them seemed pretty unconcerned about it. A few even looked happy, like Paige, who gave me a big grin, and Ashley, who flashed me the thumbs-up.

Some looked unimpressed, though.

'I'm not learning exams under some peg-legged pirate,' I heard Jasmine whisper to Tove.

I gave her my coolest look. My new-found role was very important to me. If any girls thought they could make trouble, they'd better watch out.

Chapter Ten

'The next four are Jessica front right, Paige front left, Serah back right, and Riley – uh, me – behind Paige.' I paused. 'Well, imaginary Riley. Let's go.'

I sat in a high-backed chair to the side of the studio, pleased with how strong and authoritative my voice sounded. Miss Caroline had decided we'd spend the last half of technical class going over whatever exams we wanted.

If you do jazz or lyrical or ballet, you have to take a technical class to work on – you guessed it – technique. Mostly everyone was in jazz and lyrical, so we'd already practised jazz, where I'd begun to find my feet as Miss Caroline's personal assistant. Now I was really in the swing of things. We were onto lyrical, taking turns to do a mock exam in our groups of four. Those who weren't doing the mock exam were meant to be off at the sides, practising other exams, or stretching.

Twice I'd had to tell off Violet for tapping too loud, even in bare feet. Now there was a stink of irritation floating towards me from her general direction. I ignored it. I was just doing my job, after all.

Lyrical jazz is also known as neo-classical – it's a very soft, storytelling fusion of jazz, ballet and contemporary dance. It can get quite technical, but really it's about telling a story with your body, through the song. You have to sell the emotion.

So, like I said, lyrical was the exam I was most worried about. Technically, I knew I'd hit everything, but my critiques in competitions always mention that I need to display more emotion and feeling in my movement and face. But for someone like Ellie, who maybe is just off technical perfection, the emotion isn't a problem.

So I was really looking for that in all the girls – even in their floor and standing exercises, right up to their travelling steps and the short routine.

With the standing warm-up exercises, there were a lot of body, arm and leg swings, contractions and releases, and warming up of the feet. I studied everyone, comparing them to how I would or would not have done the exercises. I was pleased when Miss Caroline called out that someone needed to extend more, or adjust this, or roll through that, and I'd had the same thought in my head.

One thing bothered me, though.

Paige was in the front row and she didn't really have any idea what was going on. She chucked a panicky look to the mirror each time the girls shifted into a new exercise, and copied them, always a beat behind.

Her actual movements were fine – turnout was solid, her feet pointed where they were meant to, and she created some pretty lines with her arms. But all of that meant nothing if she couldn't remember what came next. Marks for memory were a big part of exams, too.

The three girls finished their last standing exercise and Miss Caroline nodded.

'Not bad, girls,' she said. 'What do you think, Riley?'

'Well,' I said, and cleared my throat. I glanced at Paige, standing on the spot wringing her hands. I wondered if I should say anything. I knew she got upset and embarrassed easily.

But it wouldn't be very fair if I had criticisms for everyone but my best friends. I didn't want to be accused of playing favourites.

'Um, Paige,' I said, and shifted in my seat.

She looked up at me in surprise. I noticed Ellie look up too, from where she was stretching on the floor.

'You need to know what you're doing,' I said, as professionally as I could. 'In every single exercise you just watched what the other girls did and followed them. You need to learn the steps yourself. Plus, in the exams, we won't be performing to the mirror, like now, and you'll be up the front, so you won't actually have anyone to copy. Maybe you should practise at home so you can remember the order of things on your own.'

Paige was silent. I saw the dimple in her cheek deepen as she bit the side of her mouth, thinking. Then she looked down at her toes. 'Sorry,' she whispered. 'Okay.'

'Your lines were nice, though,' I added, to soften what I said.

Paige nodded. Miss Caroline didn't say anything. She just shuffled the girls over to the side for the travelling exercises. I did notice that she put a hand on Paige's shoulder and whispered something to her, at the end of which Paige broke out into a smile and stopped looking like I'd thrown a rotten egg in her direction.

Gosh. I'd only been trying to help.

My cheeks felt hot, and I looked down to see Ellie watching me quite peevishly

from the floor. I glared at her. I hadn't done anything wrong! If you can't take helpful criticism, then you shouldn't be a dancer. At least they got to dance, unlike me sitting here doing nothing.

'Ellie, you'll have to move from there,' I said. 'You're right in the way and Jess will trip over your leg.'

Maybe because I was feeling slightly defensive, my words sounded a bit harsh. Ellie let me know she wasn't impressed by making a face. Then she made a big act of getting up off the floor.

'Yes, sir,' she said, and marched to the side of the studio, where Ash was watching both of us. She whispered something to Ash and they both turned to look at me.

I stared straight ahead, concentrating on watching Jessica's soutenu turns.

Sorry, girls. I didn't want to be mean to

anyone. But with my beloved dancing taken away from me, this was what I had to focus on. I had a job to do. And unlike my ankle, I was determined not to stuff it up.

Chapter Eleven

I headed straight back into the studio after school the next day. It was Friday and only the seniors had lessons that afternoon. I tried to help Miss Caroline in jazz class, but I wasn't really needed. All the seniors had been dancing and taking exams for a long time and there wasn't much my ten-year-old self could teach them.

Eventually, I left the studio to have a wander around Silver Shoes and stretch my legs.

It had been a week exactly since I'd sprained my ankle, and although I knew it wasn't 100 per cent healed, it did feel a little better. Just enough to give me hope.

I really missed dancing. My head felt all busy and my heart a bit too full when I couldn't dance. I was desperate to get back out on the floor and just loosen up and work off some energy.

In the drama studio – which is the old church hall recently connected to Silver Shoes by an undercover walkway – Paige and her ballroom partner, Benji, were practising for their next competition.

I watched them through the window in the door. They were doing a fast-paced boppy dance, I think it might have been the jive, and Benji was twirling Paige round and round. They were both laughing so much they almost couldn't dance, and Paige's cheeks were a bright rosy red. Her bun, which was normally hairsprayed within an inch of its life, had come loose and her hair was flying out around her face.

She looked so cute and happy, and something burned in my chest at the thought of making her upset yesterday.

I knocked on the window, just a small tap.

Both Benji and Paige stopped and looked over at the door. Benji gave me the thumbs-up straightaway, but Paige took a step back and nervously brushed some hair off her face. I smiled my friendliest smile and gave her a little wave. After a second she smiled and waved back, and it was like the tide had come in and put out the little fire burning in my chest.

Then the ballroom teacher's face loomed out at me from the other side of the door. Everyone knew you didn't mess with Fleur.

I quickly turned on my crutch and hobbled away.

Studio two was empty, so I let myself in and came to a stop in front of the mirror. I stared at myself. Still the same Riley. Long legs, two braids, coffee-coloured skin. Puffy ankle.

I dropped the crutch beside me and pushed it away with my good foot.

Then I held myself in the starting position for the routine of the lyrical exam. I needed to practise, or at least step through it, to keep it fresh in my head, and to apply the corrections Miss Caroline had given us yesterday.

Also, I just wanted to feel a bit of the happiness and lightness dancing gave me. I knew I was giving Mr Grumpy a run for his money in the attitude department this week.

So, starting position – left arm extended, opposite leg stretched behind. Easy enough. Bend the knee, change the arms, lean forward, gently raise the back leg into développé. Still fine, because all my weight was on my good leg and my sprained ankle was the one up in the air.

But of course in the next move I had to step back onto my bad ankle and do a chaine chassé turn followed by two soutenus.

My ankle wasn't having any of that.

That's fine, I said to myself, *you haven't warmed up yet.*

So I did a slow set of relevés and pliés, and by slow, I mean *very* slow. Like, a snail could have done them quicker (if they had feet). Then I did a few tendus, dégagés and ankle rolls, carefully working through my injured ankle, stopping the range of motion or shifting the weight as soon as I felt a twinge or a pull where I shouldn't.

After that I moved to the corner and tried some simple travelling steps. My ankle felt a bit better now when I put weight on it. It cheered me up a little.

I went back to the centre of the studio and into the starting position for the lyrical routine again. This time I let my arms and upper body perform at their full range of motion and limited the amount of footwork I was doing – I did everything at a quarter of the power I normally would, in my lower half.

The steps came back to me and I imagined the music in my head. I tried to let myself feel it, to give over to the imaginary rhythm I heard.

I gave over too much though, because, before I knew it, I'd forgotten that my ankle was only working at a quarter power, and I began to dip and reach into the movements more, thinking that I was my old self.

I finished a series of stepping movements and was about to launch up into a relevé side

développé – a kind of athletic pose where you rise up on one foot, with your arms held over your head, and extend the working leg to the side, holding it in a high attitude – but just as I was coming up to the height of my rise, I felt my ankle start to give and knew I was in trouble.

I threw myself ungracefully on the floor before my ankle could roll and cause further damage. My elbows took the impact of my fall. I rolled over and lay on my back, panting.

That was close. Next thing I knew I would give myself a broken ankle. As it was, I'd have to go and get an icepack now to reduce any swelling I'd caused.

Despite all that, I was pleased with myself. I knew the limitations of what I could and couldn't do. It was a good start on my road to recovery.

Chapter Twelve

The next morning was Saturday and we had lyrical – Ellie, Paige and I were all in the class, and Ashley was around too. Her job for today was to pull up the weeds in the front gardens.

Luckily there seemed to be no weirdness between us, after that last lesson. We chatted like normal in the change rooms before class and shared a packet of jelly snakes.

'I'm so excited,' Ellie said, waving the bottom half of a snake around. 'The *Mary Poppins* show will be on in, like, three weeks! I'm going to be up on stage, singing and dancing! I can't wait till you see my solo parts – I've been working so hard on them.'

'From what I've heard, you need to work harder,' Jasmine tossed out as she passed by us on the way to the studio.

Ellie rolled her eyes and tied up her pink pullover as she stood. 'I almost can't be bothered with a comeback anymore.'

Ashley rushed to her side. 'No comebacks?' she cried. 'Are you feeling unwell? Do you need to see a doctor?'

Ellie laughed and pushed her out the door. 'Go and prune the roses,' she said. 'Save some of the thorns so I can put them in Jasmine's shoes.'

'Ellie!' gasped Paige. 'That's terrible!'

'That'll keep her on her toes,' Ashley cracked. 'See you guys later.'

I followed the other girls into the studio, trying my hardest to not rely on my crutch too much. I was hoping next week I could stash it under my bed for good.

Miss Caroline divided us up into our exam groups. She took the first group – which included Jasmine, thank god, because her last name was de Lacy – and everyone else was sent with me to studio two to run through any parts we were unsure of.

I took my place by the stereo.

'What do you guys want to run first?' I asked. 'What bits are you having trouble with?'

'I'd like to do the travelling steps, if everyone else does,' said Tove. 'I keep messing up the third set.'

I didn't really think the travelling steps were

that hard, I mean, I could have done them in my sleep. But everyone else agreed with Tove. So I found the right track and got the girls to line up in their exam groups.

'One and Three go first,' I said. 'And stop on the other side to come back left. Then Two and Four go and repeat.'

'We know, Riley,' Ellie said, only half joking. 'I think we all at least understand that part.'

'I wanted to check that everyone is clear,' I said, sitting up straighter. 'Remember last year, when Bethany got confused and went first when she should have gone second? I'm just making sure stupid mistakes like that don't happen again.'

Bethany flushed and twisted her skirt in her hands. 'I was nervous,' she muttered. 'Not stupid.'

My cheeks might have gone a little red but

I turned the volume up on the stereo and clapped for the first group to line up.

'Remember to stand in prep while you're waiting,' I called out sternly, because two of the girls weren't. 'For your turns, the right leg is out in a held tendu.'

The two girls unwillingly shifted their feet. Geez. You'd think I just asked them to do fifty sit-ups.

They launched into their first travelling step, which was a turning sequence of chaines, chassés, posés and lame ducks. I yelled out things like 'Bethany, you need to spot,' and 'Serah, that lame duck looks more like a posé,' and 'Ellie, sit lower in your chaine'.

Ellie flicked me an annoyed look as she finished the sequence and lined up again to go back left. 'I know how to squat in second, Riley,' I heard her mutter.

On the second travelling step, which

was a series of waltz steps, I banged my crutch against the chair leg and shouted out '**One** *two three,* **one** *two three,*' even louder than the music, because some of the girls had their timing really off. It frustrated me – how hard could it be to do three steps to a beat? I would have given anything to be up there, doing it with them, and they just seemed like they couldn't be bothered. So that made me bang and shout even more, trying to get the girls to listen to me. Some of them flung these stinky little looks my way, but if I didn't tell them, who would?

The third travelling step involved a switching battement jump, but the majority of the girls were having trouble with the transition. I watched them keep muddling through it and eventually I threw up my hands, stopped the music and barged into the middle of them.

'No, it's like this,' I said, and I did the step exactly as Miss Caroline had showed us, sweeping my left leg up into a battement jump, then turning my body in mid-air so I ended up facing back the way I had come. It was exhilarating. *This is how you do it,* my face said to them.

But then, of course, I landed on my bung ankle, which couldn't take the weight, so my knee buckled and I ended up on the floor.

I mean, that was embarrassing, but you know what was the worst part? No one, not even Ellie or Paige, came forward to help me. They even looked a bit gleeful that I'd ended up on my butt staring at them.

'Well, Miss Caroline never showed us that part,' Tove said, and a few of the girls tittered.

Only then did Ellie glare at them and toss her hair, grabbing Paige's arm as she bent down to me.

'Need a hand, Riles?' she asked.

Paige knelt down on my other side and put her small, cold hands under my arm to help me up. As she and Ellie pulled me to my feet, Ellie fixed each and every other girl with a look of disdain.

'Riley's *injured*, you know,' she said. 'I didn't see any of you even come near to being as good as her just then, and I'm pretty sure none of you have a sprained ankle. So why don't you all stop staring and go and practise.'

I was too mortified to even thank her as they took me back to my seat.

Chapter Thirteen

'I heard you had a bit of a topple on Saturday morning.' Miss Caroline stopped out the front of her office.

The light coming in the stained-glass windows made her face look pretty and soft, like a butterfly lady. I watched a dust mote as it wafted aimlessly in the air.

'Nothing major,' I said, shrugging my shoulders.

It was Monday afternoon, when I'd usually have ballet. I'm proud to say my latest progress was I only carried the crutch around now and used it for the hard bits, like getting up stairs.

'Nevertheless,' said Miss Caroline, 'you have to be careful. You shouldn't even be thinking about dancing until next week. If you rush to get better, you deny your injuries the process of healing. An injury isn't a quick or easy thing, Riley. It's an annoying ordeal, but unfortunately it's part and parcel of being a dancer.'

'Well, the stupid thing is I didn't even get it while I was dancing,' I said, and then I felt uncomfortable under Miss Caroline's stern, kind gaze, so I blew at the dust mote and changed the subject. 'You want me to print something else off for you, Miss Caroline?'

She handed me her USB. 'Yes,' she said. 'Just the document on the official exam uniform. I copied it on there this morning. Thirty copies would be great. Afterwards, come and find me in ballet. I need you to take note of everyone who wants a practice CD for exams.'

It was very quiet in Miss Caroline's office; all I could hear was the faraway clatter of someone typing. There was a half finished cup of tea on her desk. I pushed it to one side and inserted the USB into the computer, tapping my fingers while I waited for it to load.

Up came the familiar icons. I saw 'Exam Uniform Printout' and went to click on it. Then I stopped. My right pointer finger hovered over the mouse. I could faintly see my reflection in the computer screen, staring at the forbidden icon. The icon I shouldn't click. The icon that was none of my business.

I clicked it.

'Don't tell on me, tea,' I told the cold cup of Earl Grey. 'I'm doing this for the benefit of the other students.'

Yeah, right.

There everyone was, listed in alphabetical order. My eyes darted from the door to the screen as I hunted for the names that interested me.

My own, of course.

But a quick check revealed a blank page for Riley Nason. Obviously my injury counted me out of any critiques.

Never mind. Let's see what Miss Caroline had to say about Jasmine de Lacy.

Ew. Pretty much under every style was a heap of positive notes: 'Excellent lines, rotation and turnout has improved significantly, lovely grand battement.'

Blah, blah, blah.

Looks like Little Miss Perfect had her exams in the bag.

I hesitated only a moment before I clicked into Ellie's. I was leaning forward so far, as if my body would shield the light coming from the computer and not give me away.

You shouldn't be doing this, I told myself. But at the same time my body felt all tingly, like it was excited about my secret life as a Silver Shoes sleuth.

Ellie had some positive things written in her practice notes, too. But, to my surprise, she also had some negatives. One was what I'd already told her: she needed to get down into her plié more on the chaine. Under 'Technique' was written, 'overextends the back in barre work, funny lines, fix next session'. But it was jazz, Ellie's favourite style, that surprised me the most, because Miss Caroline had written 'in enthusiasm and energy, sometimes does not finish movements properly, so can come across as lazy.' Ellie would NOT be happy about that. She'd been bragging how easily she would ace the jazz exam.

'Hey Riley, whatcha doing?'

My skin jumped from my bones. I pushed back in the seat. I frantically clicked the 'x' at the top of the screen, and almost knocked the cold tea over in the process.

'Ashley!' I eventually said (well, really, yelled). 'What are you doing?'

'I asked first,' she joked. 'Living large in the boss's office, I see.'

My heart was pounding out of my chest. 'Miss Caroline asked me to print some stuff off for her,' I stammered.

Ashley looked at the printer, which was silent.

'There was a paper jam,' I snapped. 'What do you want?'

'Uh.' Ashley looked at me in surprise and pushed her hair out of her eyes. 'I was on my way to the costume room,' she said. 'Saw you and thought I would say hi.'

'Well, I'm busy,' I said. 'I have work to do.' I was being crabby, I know, but I was so flustered at almost being caught that I just wanted Ashley to go away so I could calm down.

'Oh,' Ashley stepped into the room. 'Need any help? The costume room is pretty much –'

'Miss Caroline asked *me* to do it,' I said haughtily, turning to the computer screen. 'Just go and do your cleaning stuff. You shouldn't be in Miss Caroline's office. It's off limits to students.'

'But you're in here,' Ashley pointed out.

'I'm her personal assistant,' I practically shouted. 'Not you! You're the cleaner!'

Ashley stared at me a moment and then a look came over her face that I'd never seen in all our months of being best friends.

I didn't like it at all. It made me feel about the size of a crumb.

'That's cool,' she said, 'I get it. I'll leave you to your important business, queen, and take my humble servant self to where I'm wanted.'

I watched her walk away and I didn't feel like a crumb anymore.

I felt like a speck of dirt instead.

Chapter Fourteen

Our age group didn't have any classes on Tuesday, so thankfully I didn't see Ellie, Ashley or Paige at the studios. It was nice to just help Miss Caroline with the younger kids. I knew things would be awkward with Ash after yesterday, and it had been bugging me since I was rude to her. We'd never had a fight and I wanted to apologise. Plus, I really wanted to talk to her about my frustration at not being able to dance – she was so good at cheering me up.

I also didn't want to see Ellie, knowing what I knew.

Should I tell her? Or should I try to show her what she was doing wrong in practice? Maybe I should say nothing, seeing as it was secret information, and I wasn't supposed to know at all? Would it give her an unfair advantage over the other girls if I told her?

I hated having a secret. It was such a miserable feeling. I knew that when I looked at Ellie, that's all I would think about. I wished I'd never opened the stupid file at all. It was hanging over my head like a bad smell.

'Curiosity killed the cat, Riley,' Nana always says to me. She'd be disappointed I'd looked at the file in the first place, and somehow that made me feel the worst. I didn't want to be a disappointment to anyone.

On Wednesday I decided to just face the music and apologise to Ash straightaway. I walked right up to my friends in the change room while they were getting ready for jazz.

'Hi guys,' I said. 'Look, no crutch!'

'That's great, Riley!' said Paige. 'Your ankle is feeling better then?'

'Oh,' said Ashley, not looking up from her packet of snakes. 'Look who's decided to lower herself to talk to us today. Haven't you got better things to do?'

The grin shrank from Paige's face and it clouded over with worry. I was so hurt by Ashley's tone, it was the coldest and meanest I'd ever heard her sound. She wouldn't even look at me! The apology I'd been about to say curled up on my tongue. I turned on my heel and left the room without another word.

Ellie caught up to me in the hall outside of the studios.

'Riley!' she panted. 'What happened back there? Are you and Ash fighting?'

'Why don't you ask her?' I said.

'But you guys never fight!' said Ellie. She reached out a hand and pulled me to a stop.

'Watch my ankle,' I growled at her.

She dropped my arm and leant away from me, her green eyes narrowing. Great. Now she was going to give me a tongue-lashing, too.

'What's wrong with you lately, Riley?' she asked. 'I know you've hurt your ankle, and that sucks, but you're being really bossy and a bit mean to everyone. Like in class . . .'

'Miss Caroline asked me to be her personal assistant!' I shouted. 'I'm just doing my job. If that means I have to be bossy and tell people they're doing something wrong, then that's what I have to do! No one's going to improve if I'm nice to them all the time and tell them they're perfect.'

'Riley –' began Ellie.

'Do you know how frustrating it is,' I continued, 'to just want to dance, and you can't, and it's all trapped inside of you, and on top of that you have to watch everyone do everything and make mistakes when I know that *I* could be up there, putting all my hard work into practice, but I can't because I have THIS.' I gasped for breath and held my foot away from my body in disgust.

'We're ten years old,' Ellie said. 'We're still learning. It's just exams, not the Olympics. If you keep being bossy and mean to us, instead of saying things nicely and helpfully –'

'Oh, be quiet!' I interrupted her. 'You're bossy and mean all the time! My nana would say that's the pot calling the kettle black! Half the girls here don't even like you.'

'What?' said Ellie. Her eyes brimmed up and she jutted out her chin.

I felt so, so bad because it takes a lot to make Ellie cry, she's pretty tough. But I had so much frustration and anger and disappointment inside that it was pushing these poisonous flames up through my throat and out of my mouth.

'And you need to work harder anyway,' I blurted. 'You over-bend your back and you don't finish off movements properly because you're so eager to show off. Maybe you should be practising instead of having a go at me!'

A tear slipped down Ellie's cheek and she wiped it away angrily. 'Is that what you think?' she asked quietly.

'No, that's, that's what . . . that's what Miss Caroline told me!' I lied.

Ellie didn't say anything but she looked absolutely crushed. Great. Now, in addition to being injured and useless, I was the biggest meanie on the planet.

'Oh, just leave me alone, Ellie!' I pushed past her and ran off and didn't stop until I found a dark corner where I slumped down and then I cried, and cried, and cried.

Chapter Fifteen

Of my three best friends, I was sure only one actually liked me, and even then I was afraid of talking to Paige in case she thought I was mean and bossy, too.

I was super sorry I'd said those things to Ellie, and that I'd been rude to Ash the day before, but I didn't know how to fix it. I could admit that I'd gone over the top with the attitude but, really, I thought they needed to be more understanding of my situation, too. They couldn't expect special privileges from me when it came to exam critiques just because I was their friend. It wasn't fair to me and it wasn't fair to the other girls.

It was so awkward in class. When I took the rest of the girls into studio one to practise the jazz exam while Miss Caroline ran through the first group, there were two sets of eyes staring at me. Not to mention Jasmine and Tove standing up the back, tittering and whispering with their hands over their mouths.

'Is it just me, or is there tension in the air today?' Jasmine drawled, while I fumbled around putting the music on.

I went to tell her to be quiet but at the last moment my shoulders drooped and I couldn't get the words out. The fire in my chest had gobbled them all up.

'It's good to see your ankle has got better, Riley,' Jasmine continued. 'Hopefully your attitude has improved along with it.'

Paige turned around angrily. 'Hopefully yours has, too,' she said, in a very un-Paige-like outburst. 'Riley's been unwell. What's your excuse?'

Jasmine was so shocked about being told off by Paige that she shut up immediately.

'First group in standing exercise positions,' I said, quietly. 'Rest of you stretching or practising on the sides.' I paused. 'Please,' I added.

Paige, her cheeks bright red, but a secret little smile on her face, went off to stretch in the corner. I saw Ashley give Paige a hearty pat on the back, and I felt very proud of Paige for speaking up, and a big rush of affection towards Ashley for making her feel good about it.

We went through the groups, one by one, but I didn't say anything, except for generic things like 'Thanks, girls,' and 'Flat backs, feet together,' to the group as a whole.

I felt extra uncomfortable when it was my friends' turn. Because I'd told Paige off last lesson for copying other people, I noticed that this time she tried very hard not to look anywhere but at the front. So she forgot a few things but, instead of looking to the other girls, she would simply bite her lip, gather her thoughts, and pick up once she'd remembered what came next.

I was so proud of her for trying, but didn't know how to say so. There was a weird kind of imaginary barrier between us.

Ashley made a point of not looking at me at all, and ignoring everything I said completely. Ellie, on the other hand, made a show of doing everything really lazily, almost daring me to correct her. We both knew that it wasn't her best work, but I bit down on my tongue and just watched the other girls.

I felt all hot and floaty at the same time, like I had a temperature. I was lost among my gloomy thoughts and I had to try really hard to not collapse and have a good old cry.

Bethany stopped in the middle of the kicking sequence in the travelling steps.

'Riley,' she said, 'do we turn to the front or back on the last backwards kick? And do we do all of the kicks on demi pointe? I've noticed that some of us are and some of us aren't.'

I blinked. I hadn't noticed that, I'd been so lost in my miserable little daze.

'Uh,' I said, 'um.'

Bethany stood there looking at me, and everyone else turned to me for confirmation, too.

I really had no clue. I couldn't for the life of me remember. I risked a quick glance at Ellie, then Ashley, but both of them avoided my gaze. Paige just gave me a little shrug when I glanced at her; she wasn't sure either. The only one who would have known for sure was Jasmine, and her group was currently in with Miss Caroline.

I had to make the call. It was my job. It was time to take command again and get my head back in the game.

'You turn to the front on the last kick,' I decided. 'And the kicks are all on flat feet.'

'Are you sure?' one girl, Opal, asked. 'I thought Miss Caroline said . . .'

I paused, just for a second. 'The kicks are all on flat feet,' I repeated, louder. 'It shows that you're grounded and your working leg is strong. Also don't forget to keep your arms out in second on the first two kicks and in the layout.' I nodded and put the music on again, signalling they were to continue.

I actually had no idea if what I'd told the girls was the right thing. It seemed my whole life revolved around having this stupid ankle injury and I didn't remember anything before it.

But it sounded correct and I stood by my decision.

Chapter Sixteen

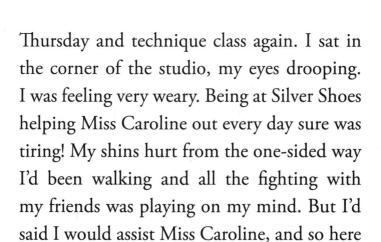

Thursday and technique class again. I sat in the corner of the studio, my eyes drooping. I was feeling very weary. Being at Silver Shoes helping Miss Caroline out every day sure was tiring! My shins hurt from the one-sided way I'd been walking and all the fighting with my friends was playing on my mind. But I'd said I would assist Miss Caroline, and so here I was.

'Riley,' she said to me as she walked over to switch songs on the iPod. 'You still with us?'

'Yes, Miss Caroline,' I said.

She eyed me down. 'You know, you've been a great help lately, but if you want to take an afternoon off, you can.'

'I'm fine.'

'How's your ankle? Have you been doing your strengthening exercises?'

'Yes,' I lied.

The truth was, I'd been so busy with my chores at Silver Shoes that I hadn't even really looked at them, much less tried them. I still thought I could do my own exercises and stop when my ankle said 'ouch'.

'Don't wear yourself down, though, I've told you this before,' she said, referring to my ability to think I can do everything. 'We want you rested, strong and confident by the time exams roll round. That's your goal.'

I just smiled and looked out at the class sadly.

'Okay,' she said. 'Now you might be feeling sprightly, but this old body needs a coffee. Do you mind making me one, Riley?'

'One sugar, not too much milk,' I said, sliding myself off the seat. 'Coming right up.'

I walked along to the teachers' room and over to the kettle. The teachers' room had lost its thrill, and I didn't even have the heart to laugh at the picture of Justin Bieber surrounded by girls that someone had taped to the fridge with the word 'Jay' scrawled next to it with an arrow.

I measured out the coffee and sugar robotically. Milk, hot water, stir.

I sighed. The last thing I wanted to do was go back into a room full of unfriendly faces. But Nana always said you should never run away from what you're scared of, you always face it. Her advice had worked out well when

I'd followed it before. So I picked the coffee mug up and made my way back to the studio.

To meet the unfriendliest face yet.

Miss Caroline's.

'Thank you,' she said, taking the mug from me and setting it down without even looking at it. 'Can I talk to you for a minute?'

Geez, what had I done now?

'Sure,' I agreed, following her into the hall.

'Riley,' she said, once we were out of earshot from the rest of the girls, although I could feel their eyes on us. 'Did you tell the girls the kicks in the travelling step for jazz were done on a flat foot?'

'Um . . . I can't really remember,' I said. 'Maybe.'

'Well, that isn't right. The kicks are done on demi. All of them. And you turn to the back, not the front. I appreciate you helping me out, but you can't go telling the girls the wrong thing. It confuses them so close to exams, and they'll get a lot of points taken off if they do the step incorrectly, all because of something you've told them.'

'I didn't do it on purpose!' I said defensively. 'I . . . thought it was done on flat feet,' I finished lamely.

'The whole point of the kicking step is to show strength and balance and turnout,' Miss Caroline said. 'Demi pointe is crucial for that. You know that, Riley. I wouldn't have let you run through exams with them if I thought you were unsure yourself.'

'I just forgot!' I protested. My voice cracked on the last word and I had to suck my breath in, loudly. Why was everyone picking on me! All I ever did was try to help!

'Well then, you should have checked with me,' Miss Caroline said, a little kinder. 'Never just guess. Always be sure.'

Shaking my head, I bit my lip, crossed my arms and looked away.

Miss Caroline put a friendly hand on my arm. 'Why don't you go and help Billie with the tinies,' she said. 'She's not feeling very well today. And it might be a bit of fun for you.'

Great. So now I'd been dumped down to helping out with the tinies. The unfairness of everything was building up and up in my chest. The flames were roaring now. I didn't even thank Miss Caroline. I just turned on my heel and stomped as best I could into the studio next door.

I couldn't do anything right.

Chapter Seventeen

When I stepped through the door, I was greeted with angelic faces and cute little tutus. But the fire in my chest was burning away all the nice feelings I had, so I couldn't even smile. I must have seemed like the wicked witch of the west to the tinies.

'Riley! My saviour.' Billie stumbled over to me, coughing and covering her nose with about ten tissues. She really didn't look well, even her brightly coloured hair seemed to have faded. 'Can you take the tinies for a bit?' she gasped. 'It's beginner's ballet. I just need to go and get . . . something . . . for this head.'

'Um . . .' Taking the tinies was the last thing I felt like doing right now.

'Girls,' rasped Billie, 'this is Riley. She'll do all the positions and some twirls with you. Be nice to her. I'll be back to check on my ballerinas in a bit.' She pushed her way out of the studio. 'Thanks, Riley,' she added.

I blinked at the door as it swung shut. Then I turned around to see all these faces looking up at me, waiting for me to teach them how to hold their arms and place their legs, when I couldn't even control the feelings whirling around inside my body.

I didn't know what to say or do. It felt like an impossible task, so I just stared at them.

'Hello,' said one little girl with blonde pigtails. 'My name's Jessie.'

I gaped at her.

'With Miss Billie we're doing first and second positions . . . and all the others,' she told me helpfully.

Fantastic. Now four-year-olds had to tell me what to do.

'Yes. All right,' I said.

'The music is ready to go,' she added. 'You just have to press play.'

I did just that and some carousel-sounding soundtrack came on. The little girls started jumping about. They looked so happy and I was so miserable. The flames in my chest leapt higher and made my throat all dry and parched.

'Okay.' I cleared my throat. The tinies kept jumping about. 'Okay, girls,' I said, a little louder, trying to keep the wobble out of my voice. 'First position. Who remembers?'

They all looked at me expectantly. Gosh. I was meant to show them. What was first position? For the life of me I couldn't think what it even meant.

Feet turned out. Arms in front. I forced my body into the sloppiest version of first position I'd ever done.

Focus, Riley, focus. But I couldn't. I just had to get out, and away.

I heard the door to the studio crack open. Thank God. Billie was back.

But it wasn't Billie. Instead, Paige's sweet, friendly face was looking at me, worry in her blue eyes.

'Hi girls,' she sang to the tinies. 'Lovely first positions!' They all beamed at her.

Paige hurried over to me. 'Are you okay?' she asked. 'Miss Caroline sent me to quickly check on you.'

I looked at her, and I knew I was about

to cry. Someone actually being nice to me was the hardest thing of all. I was going to bawl and I had to leave the studio.

'Please help me, Paige,' I said.

Paige nodded. 'Go and get a glass of water,' she said, squeezing my arm. 'I'll take over from here.'

I swallowed and stumbled out.

'Okay, cuties,' I heard Paige say, 'Riley is just going to check in on Miss Billie, so Miss Paige is going to help you today. Now, who can show me a nice second position?'

I legged it to the drama studio as fast as my injured ankle would take me. Once I was there, I sat near the mirror in silence for a very long time, thinking all my bad thoughts and feeling my chest get bigger and bigger, and hotter and hotter.

Then I cried: about my ankle and my friends, and all the unfairness of the last two weeks. About all the mean things I'd done just because I was frustrated, about the ache in my heart because I couldn't dance, and when all that was out, I swiped at my tears and pushed my hair back and got up to face the mirror.

And then I started jumping and leaping about, and throwing myself into some crazy kind of Riley dance because I thought that was the only way I could truly get my feelings out. I pushed through the pain in my ankle and I beat away my rasping breath, and I fought for the feelings that dance had always given me – power, beauty, focus, strength.

I didn't stop until three girls appeared in the doorway.

Ellie, Ashley, and Paige.

Chapter Eighteen

'Riley, what are you doing?' cried Paige, rushing over to me. 'You know you're not meant to be dancing on your ankle.'

Ashley and Ellie shuffled in after her slowly.

I collapsed on the floor and took in some big, heaving breaths. My ankle tingled a little, like it was scolding me. But my chest was wonderfully light and cool – all the flames had gone. There was perhaps a small piece of coal in there, barely warm. But my head, and my heart, felt clear.

'Sorry for dumping the tinies class on you,' I said to Paige.

'That's fine,' said Paige, kneeling down next to me. 'I'm more worried about you. You looked terrible back there.'

'It's been a rough couple of weeks,' I said, avoiding the desire to look at Ellie and Ash. But then I decided that, no, it wasn't doing me any good to keep everything all bottled up, so I pushed on.

'Miss Caroline made me her personal assistant and I thought that was really cool,' I said, poking softly at my bad ankle, 'because it let me be at Silver Shoes and stay in-the-know. I only ever wanted to do a good job. But some people thought I was being mean and bossy when I was just trying to help.'

'You *were* being mean and bossy,' Ellie muttered. But then she sighed, and slumped down on the floor next to me. 'But I guess I can be too when something's bothering me.' She tossed her hair and plucked at her pink tights. 'Also, you were right about what you said, you know, about my back arching and not finishing off movements and stuff. Miss Caroline mentioned something about it today.'

'Oh?' I said, trying to look surprised.

'Yeah,' said Ellie. 'I know you were just trying to help when you told me.'

I pulled on my braids. 'But I probably could have told you in a nicer way,' I admitted, before turning to Paige. 'Also, that time in the studio. I could have said those things too without being mean. Or, like, not in front of the whole class. I never wanted to embarrass you.'

'I know you didn't,' said Paige. 'Also I do rely too much on other people in the exams.

I just needed to be told because I was fooling myself that I was fine. But I've been trying really hard this week to remember everything on my own.'

'And you're doing great,' Ellie added, smiling at her. 'You always need to trust yourself more, Paige. You're just as good as everyone else.'

'I'm working on it,' said Paige.

There was a silence while everyone wondered if Ash and I were ever going to speak to each other.

Finally I decided, for my own happiness, to break it.

'Look, Ash,' I began.

'Hey, Riles,' she said at the same time.

Finally we caught each other's eye. Then she started to grin, the big, jokey, Ashley smile that was so infectious. I think it's what I love about her best.

'You caught me on a bad day that time in Miss Caroline's office,' I said. 'I was feeling yuck 'cause I missed dancing and I took it out on you. And I guess I got carried away with being a personal assistant. It's just that it made me feel useful and important, while having an injury made me feel exactly the opposite. So I'm really sorry if I was rude.'

'Ah, well,' said Ash. 'It's like my dad says – never interrupt a man at his work. Except you're not a man. Well, I don't think so, anyway.' She prodded me with her toe. 'I was a bit much with the attitude too, in the change room. Sorry about that.'

'Yeah, you gave Jasmine a run for her money.' I giggled.

Laughing, Ashley threw herself on me in a big hug. 'Whatever, Riles. You've missed me, attitude or not.' Untangling herself from me, she patted my leg. 'Now that all the emotional stuff is out of the way, what about this ankle? You were dancing like your old self just then. So it's feeling better? Back in the exam race?'

'It is feeling better,' I said happily. 'Definitely not 100 per cent, and I probably shouldn't have been dancing like that. But . . . it did make me remember how much I love dancing, and how soon I want to get back to it. I think I need to amp up my recovery program.'

'You haven't been doing your strengthening exercises, have you?' Paige asked.

'Not really,' I said. 'I've just been trusting my own instincts. But I'm no doctor.' I looked round at all of them. 'Which is why I need you guys to help me and make sure I'm doing everything I absolutely can to get this ankle right.'

'A chance to be bossy,' Ellie joked. 'Apparently, I'm quite good at that.'

I stood, pulling the girls up with me. 'Will you come with me to see Miss Caroline, now? I want to ask her advice on the best things to do for my ankle so it's right for exams.' I gave an embarrassed cough. 'And I'll actually listen this time.'

'You want me to piggyback you there, ol' Peg Leg?' asked Ash.

'I can go and get a wheelbarrow,' said Ellie.

'I think there was a horse and cart out front,' added Paige.

'All your bad jokes are hurting my brain,' I groaned.

But inside, I was so, so happy. I had my friends back, and soon, if I did the right things, I would have my ankle back, too.

And then I would be able to dance again.

I was ready to ace exams.

So You Think You Know Modern and Lyrical Dance?

Fun facts about modern, contemporary, lyrical and neo-classical dance:

It's easy to get confused about what exactly modern or lyrical dance is, when it has changed, evolved and been influenced by so much in the past one hundred years. So here's a simple outline of the main differences in styles.

Modern or contemporary dance:

- A natural, often instinctive way of movement that allows you to use creative lines and body weight to produce distinct ways of moving
- Lines are often abstract or isolated from other parts of the body
- Movement is centred around a central axis

- Movements often begin with one body part, transitioning into another
- Fall and release, movement and suspension, isolations and contractions, and travelling steps done in plié are a key to this style of dance
- A big reason for the growth in popularity of the modern dance in the early 1900s is that it signified a rebellion against the rigid, uniform lines of classical ballet

Lyrical or neo-classical dance:
- The fusion of ballet and jazz technique, which is held together by the expression of the dancer's inner emotion
- Traditional lines taken from the classical style
- Choreography usually has movements that flow very naturally and smoothly into each other, with little or no stopping, or moments of stillness

- Movements are flowing, carving, or arcing with emphasis on pathways merging into one another
- Focus on how the dancer expresses themselves, with less concentration on precision and more on individual style
- Connection between music and movement is central, which means the audience can easily understand and connect to the dancer, the choreography, and the music

Popular modern and lyrical dancers
- Maddie Ziegler
- Mia Michaels
- Lady Gaga
- Martha Graham
- Isadora Duncan
- Alvin Ailey
- Cirque du Soleil

Best of modern and lyrical on YouTube

- *Chandelier* – Sia
- *Wandering Star* – Polica
- *Bad Romance* – Lady Gaga
- *White Nights* – Oh Land
- *Lamentation* – Martha Graham
- *Calling You* – Travis and Heidi *(So You Think You Can Dance?)*
- *Dancing* – Lacey and Kameron *(So You Think You Can Dance?)*

Glossary

Hey guys,

First of all, I've got to say, you should never dance when you're injured! Always tell an adult and ask for help if you think you might have hurt yourself. Trust me, I Iearned the hard way! Here are some terms you might come across whether you dance lyrical, neo-classical, or contemporary. Strong technique is always the best foundation for these styles of dance, but also think about selling the mood, emotion, or feel of the song. The best dancers always dance from their heart!

Love, Riley

barrel jump a jump where you completely turn around with legs in bent position

chaine chassé a turning sequence; the first turn is in a deep plié and the chassé turns that follow are performed in a three-step sliding motion, where one foot 'chases' and displaces the other

contraction a movement based on breath inhalation and exhalation, the foundation of contemporary dance. At its most basic, the body jerks inwards, like being punched in the stomach!

dégagé when you shift the weight from one foot to the other

développé when you unfold one leg in the air

isolations movement separating one part of the body from the other parts

lame duck turn when you fall onto the right leg, then swing the left leg around to replace the right, and move the right leg up to the knee. The turn is done away from the supporting leg.

layout a very dramatic movement where you extend one leg out and arch your back at the same time

pas de bourrée a travelling or transitional step done on the points of the toes that moves back, side, then front

plié when you bend the knees in any of the five positions, with your body upright

posé turn a travelling step where you step out onto demi pointe or pointe, keeping a straight knee, with the other leg in passé position

preparation the step or position you use before you go into a jump, turn, leap, extended sequence etc. It is very important for correct technique and avoiding injury (like me!)

relevé a rising movement where you roll onto your toes from a flat foot

saut de basque a turn where the leading foot is stepped on and the other leg is brushed forward and jumped on

soutenu when you step to parallel second in plié, and then pull the second leg in to meet the preparation leg as the turn is done with both feet in relevé

tendu when you slide your foot out in pointe to the front, side or back, lifting your heel off the floor

tombé when you step out into second in preparation for a travelling step

turning jeté a jeté that is turned into through a plié; coming into a 360-degree rotation on your turn, the momentum is used to jeté forward

turnout a rotation of the leg that comes from the hips, causing the knee and foot to turn outward, away from the centre of the body

waltz step in jazz or ballet, a travelling step that moves forwards and is done to the *one* two three waltz rhythm

About the Author

Samantha-Ellen Bound has been an actor, dancer, teacher, choreographer, author, bookseller, scriptwriter and many other things besides. She has published and won prizes for her short stories and scripts, but children's books are where her heart lies. Dancing is one of her most favourite things in the whole world. She splits her time between Tasmania, Melbourne, and living in her own head.

Silver Shoes

And All That Jazz

SAMANTHA-ELLEN BOUND

Silver Shoes

Hit the Streets

SAMANTHA-ELLEN BOUND

Silver Shoes

Breaking Pointe

SAMANTHA-ELLEN BOUND

Silver Shoes

Dance Till You Drop

SAMANTHA-ELLEN BOUND

Silver Shoes

Broadway Baby

SAMANTHA-ELLEN BOUND

Silver Shoes

Lights, Camera, Dance!

SAMANTHA-ELLEN BOUND

Silver Shoes

Rhythm and Blues

SAMANTHA-ELLEN BOUND

Silver Shoes

Studio Showdown

SAMANTHA-ELLEN BOUND

COLLECT THEM ALL!